Gitanjali

Rabindranath Tagore

MG BOOKS
NEW DELHI (INDIA)

Gitanjali

Published by

MG BOOKS

An Imprint of

MAANU GRAPHICS

MAANU GRAPHICS

(PUBLISHERS OF GENERAL BOOKS)

5FF, Ganpati Bhawan, 21 Ansari Road,
Darya Ganj, New Delhi-110002
Ph: 65285220, 64138266
E-mail : maanugraphics@yahoo.com
mgbooks.maanu@yahoo.com

Printed at

Satyam Enterprises, Delhi

CONTENTS

THE NOBEL PRIZE ACCEPTANCE SPEECH

I AM glad that I have been able to come at last to your country and that I may use this opportunity for expressing my gratitude to you for the honour you have done to me by acknowledging my work and rewarding me by giving me the Nobel Prize.

I remember the afternoon when I received the cablegram from my publisher in England that the prize had been awarded to me. I was staying then at the school Shantiniketan, about which I suppose you know. At that moment we were taking a party over to a forest near by the school, and when I was passing by the telegram office and the post office, a man came running to us and held up the telegraphic message. I had also an English visitor with me in the same carriage. I did not think that the message was of any importance, and I just put it into my pocket, thinking that I would read it, when I reached my destination. But my visitor supposed he knew the contents, and he urged me to read it, saying that it contained an important message. And I opened and read the message, which I could hardly believe. 1 first thought that possibly the telegraphic language was not quite correct and that I might misread the meaning of it, but at last I felt certain about it. And you can well understand how rejoicing it was for my boys at the school and for the teachers. What touched me more deeply than anything else was that these boys who loved me and for whom I had the deepest love felt proud of the honour that had been awarded to him for whom they had feeling of reverence, and I realized that my countrymen would share with me the honour which had been awarded to myself.

The rest of the afternoon passed away in this manner, and when the night came I sat upon the terrace alone, and I asked myself the question what the reason could be of my poems being accepted and honoured by the West – in spite of my belonging to a different race, parted and separated by seas and mountains from the children of the West And I can assure you that it was not with a feeling of exaltation but with a searching of the heart that I questioned myself, and I felt humble at that moment.

I remember how my life's work developed from the time when I was very young. When I was about 25 years I used to live in utmost seclusion in the solitude of an obscure Bengal village by the river Ganges in a boat-house. The wild ducks which came during the time of autumn from the Himalayan lakes were my only living companions, and in that solitude I seem to have drunk in the open space like wine overflowing with sunshine, and the murmur of the river used to speak to me and tell me the secrets of nature.

And I passed my days in the solitude dreaming and giving shape to my dream in poems and studies and sending out my thoughts to the Calcutta public through the magazines and other papers. You can well understand that it was a life quite different from the life of the West. I do not know if any of your Western poets or writers do pass the greatest part of their young days in such absolute seclusion. I am almost certain that it cannot be possible and that seclusion itself has no place in the Western world.

And my life went on like this. I was an obscure individual – to most of my countrymen in those days. I mean that my name was hardly known outside my own province, but I was quite content with that obscurity, which protected me from the curiosity of the crowds.

And then came a time when my heart felt a longing to come out of that solitude and to do some work for my human fellow-beings, and not merely give shapes to my dreams and meditate deeply on the problems of life, but try to give expression to my ideas through some definite work, some definitive service for my fellow-beings.

And the one thing, the one work which came to my mind was to teach children. It was not because I was specially fitted for this work of teaching, for I have not had myself the full benefit of a regular education. For some time I hesitated to take upon myself this task, but I felt that as I had a deep love for nature I had naturally love for children also. My object in starting this institution was to give the children of men full freedom of joy, of life and of communion with nature. I myself had suffered when I was young through the impediments which were inflicted upon most boys while they attended school and I have had to go through the machine of education which crushes the joy and freedom of life for which children have such insatiable thirst. And my object was to give freedom and joy to children of men.

And so I had a few boys around me, and I taught them, and I tried to make them happy. I was their playmate. I was their companion. I shared their life, and I felt that I was the biggest child of the party. And we all grew up together in this atmosphere of freedom. The vigour and the joy of the children, their chats and songs filled the air with a spirit of delight, which I drank every day I was there. And in the evening during the sun-set hour I often used to sit alone watching the trees of the shadowing avenue, and in the silence of the afternoon I could hear distinctly the voices of the children coming up in the air, and it seemed to me that these shouts and songs and glad voices were like those trees, which come out from the heart of the earth like fountains of life towards the bosom of the infinite sky. And it symbolized, it brought before my mind the whole cry of human life all expressions of joy and aspirations of men rising from the heart of Humanity up to this sky. I could see that, and I knew that we also, the grown-up children, send up our cries of aspiration to the Infinite. I felt it in my heart of hearts.

In this atmosphere and in this environment I used to write my poems Gitanjali, and I sang them to myself in the midnight under the glorious stars of the Indian sky. And in the early morning and in the afternoon glow of sun-set I used to write these songs till a day came when I felt impelled to come out once again and meet the heart of the large world.

I could see that my coming out from the seclusion of my life among these joyful children and doing my service to my fellow creatures was only a prelude to my pilgrimage to a larger world. And I felt a great desire to come out and come into touch with the Humanity of the West, for I was conscious that the present age belongs to the Western man with his superabundance of energy.

He has got the power of the whole world, and his life is overflowing all boundaries and is sending out its message to the great future. And I felt that I must before I die come to the West and meet the man of the secret shrine where the Divine presence has his dwelling, his temple. And I thought that the Divine man with all his powers and aspirations of life is dwelling in the West.

And so I came out. After my Gitanjali poems had been written in Bengali I translated those poems into English, without having any desire to have them published, being diffident of my mastery of that language, but I had – the manuscript with me when I came out to the West. And you know that the British public, when these poems were put before them, and those who had the opportunity of reading them in manuscript before, approved of them. I was accepted, and the heart of the West opened without delay.

And it was a miracle to me who had lived for fifty years far away from activity, far away from the West, that I should be almost in a moment accepted by the West as one of its own poets. It was surprising to me, but I felt that possibly this had its deeper significance and that those years which I had spent in seclusion, separated from the life and the spirit of the West, had brought with them a deeper feeling of rest, serenity and feeling of the eternal, and that these were exactly the sentiments that were needed by the Western people with their overactive life, who still in their heart of hearts have a thirst for the peace, for the infinite peace. My fitness was that training which my muse had from my young days in the absolute solitude of the beaches of the Ganges. The peace of those years had been stored in my nature so that I could bring it out and hold it up to the man of the West, and what I offered to him was accepted gratefully.

I know that I must not accept that praise as my individual share. It is the East in me which gave to the West. For is not the East the mother of spiritual Humanity and does not the West, do not the children of the West amidst their games and plays when they get hurt, when they get famished and hungry, turn their face to that serene mother, the East? Do they not expect their food to come from her, and their rest for the night when they are tired? And are they to be disappointed.

Fortunately for me I came in that very moment when the West had turned her face again to the East and was seeking for some nourishment. Because I represented the East I got my reward from my Eastern friends.

And I can assure you that the prize which you have awarded to me was not wasted upon myself. I as an individual had no right to accept it, and therefore I have made use of it for others. I have dedicated it to our Eastern children and students. But then it is like a seed which is put into the earth and comes up again to those who have sown it, and for their benefit it is producing fruits. I have used this money which I got from you for establishing and maintaining the university which I started lately, and it seemed to me, that this university should be a place where Western students might come and meet their Eastern brethren and when they might work together in the pursuit of truth and try to find the treasures that have lain hidden in the East for centuries and work out the spiritual resources of the East, which are necessary for all Humanity.

I can remind you of a day when India had her great university in the glorious days of her civilization. When a light is lighted it can not be held within a short range. It is for the whole world. And India had her civilization with all its splendours and wisdom and wealth. It could not use it for its own children only. It had to open its gates in hospitality to all races of men. Chinese and Japanese and Persians and all different races of men, came, and they had their opportunity of gaining what was best in India, her best offering of all times and to all Humanity. And she offered it generously. You know the traditions of our country are never to accept any material fees from the students in return to the teaching, because we consider in India that he who has the knowledge has the responsibility to impart it to the students. It is not merely for the students to come and ask it from the master, but it is the master who must fulfil his mission of life by offering the best gift which he has to all who may need it And thus it was that need of self-expression, of giving what had been stored in India and offering the best thing that she has in herself that made it possible and was the cause and the origin of these universities that were started in the different provinces of India.

And I feel that what we suffer from in the present day is no other calamity but this calamity of obscurity, of seclusion, that we have missed our opportunity of offering hospitality to Humanity and asking the world to share the best things we have got. We lost our confidence in our own civilization for over a century, when we came into contact with the Western races with their material superiority over the Eastern Humanity and Eastern culture, and in the educational establishments no provision was made for our own culture. And for over a century our students have been brought up in utter ignorance of the worth of their own civilization of the past. Thus we did not only lose touch of the great which lay hidden in our own inheritance, but also the great honour of being able to contribute to the civilization of Humanity, to have opportunity of giving what we have and not merely begging from others, not merely borrowing culture and living like eternal schoolboys.

But the time has come when we must not waste such our opportunities. We must try to do our best to bring out what we have, and not go from century to century, from land to land and display our poverty before others. We know what we have to be proud of, what we have inherited from our ancestors, and such opportunity of giving should not be lost – not only for the sake of our people, but for the sake of Humanity.

That is the reason, and that led me to the determination to establish an international institution where the Western and Eastern students could meet and share the common feast of spiritual food.

And thus I am proud to say that your awarding me the prize has made some contribution to this great object which I had in my mind. This has made me come out once again to the West, and I have come to ask you, to invite you to the feast which is waiting for you in the far East. I hope that my invitation will not be rejected. I have visited different countries of Europe, and I have accepted from them an enthusiastic welcome. That welcome has its own meaning, that the West has need of the East, as the East has need of the West, and so the time has come when they should meet.

I am glad that I belong to this great time, this great age, and I am glad that I have done some work to give expression to this great age, when the East and the West are coming together. They are proceeding towards each other. They are coming to meet each other. They have got their invitation to meet each other and join hands in building up a new civilization and the great culture of the future.

I feel certain that through my writing some such idea has reached you, even if obscurely through the translation, some idea which belongs both to the East and the West, some idea which proceeding from the East has been able to come to the West and claim its rest here, its dwelling, and to be able to receive its welcome, and has been accepted by the West. And if in my writings I have been fortunate enough to be able to interpret the voice of the need of the time I am deeply thankful to you for giving me this glorious opportunity. The acknowledgment I got from Sweden has brought me and my work before the Western public, though I can assure you that it has also given me some trouble. It has broken through the seclusion which I have been accustomed to.

It has brought me out before the great public to which I have never been accustomed. And the adjustment has not been yet made. I shrink in my heart when I stand before the great concourse of Humanity in the West. I have not yet been accustomed to accept the great gift of your praise and your admiration in the manner in which you have given it to me. And I feel ashamed and shy when standing before you – I do so now. But I will only say that I am thankful to God that he has given me this great opportunity, that I have been an instrument to bring together, to unite the hearts of the East and the West. And I must to the end of my life carry on that mission. I must do all that I can. The feeling of resentment between the East and the West must be pacified. I must do something, and with that one object I have started this institution.

I do not think that it is the spirit of India to reject anything, reject any race, reject any culture. The spirit of India has always proclaimed the ideal of unity. This ideal of unity never rejects anything, any race, or any culture. It comprehends all, and it has been the highest aim of our spiritual exertion to be able to penetrate all things with one soul, to comprehend all things as they are, and not to keep out anything in the whole universe – to comprehend all things with sympathy and love. This is the spirit of India. Now, when in the present time of political unrest the children of the same great India cry for rejection of the West I feel hurt. I feel that it is a lesson which they have received from the west. Such is not our mission. India is there to unite all human races. Because of that reason in India we have not been given the unity of races. Our problem is the race problem which is the problem of all Humanity. We have Dravidians, we have Mohammedans, we have Hindoos and all different sects and communities of men in India. Therefore, no superficial bond of political unity can appeal to us, can satisfy us, can ever be real to us.

We must go deeper down. We must discover the most profound unity, the spiritual unity between the different races. We must go deeper down to the spirit of man and find out the great bond of unity, which is to be found in all human races. And for that we are well equipped. We have inherited the immortal works of our ancestors, those great writers who proclaimed the religion of unity and sympathy, in say: He who sees all beings as himself, who realizes all beings as himself, knows Truth. That has once again to be realized, not only by the children of the East but also by the children of the West. They also have to be reminded of these great immortal truths.

Man is not to fight with other human races, other human individuals, but his work is to bring about reconciliation and Peace and to restore the bonds of friendship and love. We are not like fighting beasts. It is the life of self which is predominating in our life, the self which is creating the seclusion, giving rise to sufferings, to jealousy and hatred, to political and commercial competition. All these illusions will vanish, if we go down to the heart of the shrine, to the love and unity of all races.

For that great mission of India I have started this university. I ask you now, when I have this opportunity, I invite you to come to us and join hands with us and not to leave this institution merely to us, but let your own students and learned men come to us and help us to make this university to a common institution for the

East and the West may they give the contributions of their lives and may we all together make it living and representative of the undivided Humanity of the world.

For this I have come to you. I ask you this and I claim it of you in the name of the unity of men, and in the name of love, and in the name of God. I ask you to come. I invite you.

26 May 1921,

Stockholm

GITANJALI

I

Thou hast made me endless, such is thy pleasure. This frail vessel thou emptiest again and again, and fillest it ever with fresh life.

This little flute of a reed thou hast carried over hills and dales, and hast breathed through it melodies eternally new.

At the immortal touch of thy hands my little heart loses its limits in joy and gives birth to utterance ineffable.

Thy infinite gifts come to me only on these very small hands of mine. Ages pass, and still thou pourest, and still there is room to fill.

II

When thou commandest me to sing, it seems that my heart would break with pride; and I look to thy face, and tears come to my eyes.

All that is harsh and dissonant in my life melts into one sweet harmony — and my adoration spreads wings like a glad bird on its flight across the sea.

I know thou takest pleasure in my singing. I know that only as a singer I come before thy presence.

I touch by the edge of the far-spreading wing of my song thy feet which I could never aspire to reach.

Drunk with the joy of singing I forget myself and call thee friend who art my lord.

III

I know not how thou singest, my master! I ever listen in silent amazement.

The light of thy music illumines the world. The life breath of thy music runs from sky to sky. The holy stream of thy music breaks through all stony obstacles and rushes on.

My heart longs to join in thy song, but vainly struggles for a voice. I would speak, but speech breaks not into song, and I cry out baffled. Ah, thou hast made my heart captive in the endless meshes of thy music, my master!

IV

Life of my life, I shall ever try to keep my body pure, knowing that thy living touch is upon all my limbs.

I shall ever try to keep all untruths out from my thoughts, knowing that thou art that truth which has kindled the light of reason in my mind.

I shall ever try to drive all evils away from my heart and keep my love in flower, knowing that thou hast thy seat in the inmost shrine of my heart.

And it shall be my endeavour to reveal thee in my actions, knowing it is thy power gives me strength to act.

V

I ask for a moment's indulgence to sit by thy side. The works that I have in hand I will finish afterwards.

Away from the sight of thy face my heart knows no rest nor respite, and my work becomes an endless toil in a shoreless sea of toil.

To-day the summer has come at my window with its sighs and murmurs; and the bees are plying their minstrelsy at the court of the flowering grove.

Now it is time to sit quiet, face to face with thee, and to sing dedication of life in this silent and overflowing leisure.

VI

Pluck this little flower and take it. Delay not! I fear lest it droop and drop into the dust

It may not find a place in thy garland, but honour it with a touch of pain from thy hand and pluck it. I fear lest the day end before I am aware, and the time of offering go by.

Though its colour be not deep and its smell be faint, use this flower in thy service and pluck it while there is time.

VII

My song has put off her adornments. She has no pride of dress and decoration. Ornaments would mar our union; they would come between thee and me; their jingling would drown thy whispers.

My poet's vanity dies in shame before thy sight 0 master poet, .1 have sat down at thy feet. Only let me make my life simple and straight, like a flute of reed for thee to fill with music.

VIII

The child, who is decked with prince's robes and who has jewelled chains round his neck loses all pleasure in his play; his dress hampers him at every step.

In fear that it may be frayed, or stained with dust he keeps himself from the world, and is afraid even to move.

Mother, it is no gain, thy bondage of finery, if it keep one shut off from the healthful dust of the earth, if it rob one of the right of entrance to the great fair of common human life.

IX

O fool, to try to carry thyself upon thy own shoulders! O beggar, to come to beg at thy own door!

Leave all thy burdens on his hands who can bear all, and never look behind in regret.

Thy desire at once puts out the light from the lamp it touches with its breath. It is unholy — take not thy gifts through its unclean hands. Accept only what is offered by sacred love.

X

Here is thy footstool and there rest thy feet where live the poorest, and lowliest, and lost.

When I try to bow to thee, my obeisance cannot reach down to the depth where thy feet rest among the poorest, and lowliest, and lost.

Pride can never approach to where thou walkest in the clothes of the humble among the poorest, and lowliest, and lost.

My heart can never find its way to where thou keepest company with the companionless among the poorest, the lowliest, and the lost.

XI

Leave this chanting and singing and telling of beads! Whom dost thou worship in this lonely dark corner of a temple with doors all shut Open thine eyes and see thy God is not before thee!

He is there where the tiller is tilling the hard ground and where the pathmaker is breaking stones. He is with them in sun and in shower, and his garment is covered with dust. Put off thy holy mantle and even like him come down on the dusty soil!

Deliverance? Where is this deliverance to be found? Our master himself has joyfully taken upon him the bonds of creation; he is bound with us all for ever.

Come out of thy meditations and leave aside thy flowers and incense! What harm is there if thy clothes become tattered and stained? Meet him and stand by him in toil and in sweat of thy brow.

XII

The time that my journey takes is long and the way of it long.

I came out on the chariot of the first gleam of light, and pursued my voyage through the wildernesses of worlds leaving my track on many a star and planet.

It is the most distant course that comes nearest to thyself, and that training is the most intricate which leads to the utter simplicity of a tune.

The traveller has to knock at every alien door to come to his own, and one has to wander through all the outer worlds to reach the innermost shrine at the end.

My eyes strayed far and wide before I shut them and said, "Here art thou!"

The question and the cry, "Oh, where?" melt into tears of a thousand streams and deluge the world with the flood of the assurance, "I am!"

XIII

The song that I came to sing remains unsung to this day.

I have spent my days in stringing and in unstringing my instrument.

The time has not come true, the words have not been rightly set; only there is the agony of wishing in my heart.

The blossom has not opened; only the wind is sighing by.

I have not seen his face, nor have I listened to his voice; only I have heard his gentle footsteps from the road before my house.

The livelong day has passed in spreading his seat on the floor; but the lamp has not been lit and I cannot ask him into my house.

I live in the hope of meeting with him; but this meeting is not yet.

XIV

My desires are many and my cry is pitiful, but ever didst thou save me by hard refusals; and this strong mercy has been wrought into my life through and through.

Day by day thou art making me worthy of the simple, great gifts that thou gavest to me unasked — this sky and the light, this body and the life and the mind — saving me from perils of overmuch desire.

There are times when I languidly linger and times when I awaken and hurry in search of my goal; but cruelly thou hidest thyself from before me.

Day by day thou art making me worthy of thy full acceptance by refusing me ever and anon, saving me from perils of weak, uncertain desire.

XV

I am here to sing thee songs. In this hall of thine I have a corner seat.

In thy world I have no work to do; my useless life can only break out in tunes without a purpose.

When the hour strikes for thy silent worship at the dark temple of midnight, command me, my master, to stand before thee to sing.

When in the morning air the golden harp is tuned, honour me, commanding my presence.

XVI

I have had my invitation to this world's festival, and thus my life has been blessed. My eyes have seen and my ears have heard.

It was my part at this feast to play upon my instrument, and I have done all I could.

Now, I ask, has the time come at last when I may go in and see thy face and offer thee my silent salutation?

XVII

I am only waiting for love to give myself up at last into his hands. That is why it is so late and why I have been guilty of such omissions.

They come with their laws and their codes to bind me fast; but I evade them ever, for I am only waiting for love to give myself up at last into his hands.

People blame me and call me heedless; I doubt not they are right in their blame.

The market day is over and work is all done for the busy. Those who came to call me in vain have gone back in anger. I am only waiting for love to give myself up at last into his hands.

XVIII

Clouds heap upon clouds and it darkens. Ah, love, why dost thou let me wait outside at the door all alone?

In the busy moments of the noontide work I am with the crowd, but on this dark lonely day it is only for thee that I hope.

If thou showest me not thy face, if thou leavest me wholly aside, I know not how I am to pass these long, rainy hours.

I keep gazing on the far-away gloom of the sky, and my heart wanders wailing with the restless wind.

XIX

If thou speakest not I will fill my heart with thy silence and endure it. I will keep still and wait like the night with starry vigil and its head bent low with patience.

The morning will surely come, the darkness will vanish, and thy voice pour down in golden streams breaking through the sky.

Then thy words will take wing in songs from every one of my birds' nests, and thy melodies will break forth in flowers in all my forest groves.

XX

On the day when the lotus bloomed, alas, my mind was straying, and I knew it not. My basket was empty and the flower remained unheeded.

Only now and again a sadness fell upon me, and I started up from my dream and felt a sweet trace of a strange fragrance in the south wind.

That vague sweetness made my heart ache with longing and it seemed to me that it was. the eager breath of the summer seeking for its completion.

I knew not then that it was so near, that it was mine, and that this perfect sweetness had blossomed in the depth of my own heart.

XXI

I must launch out my boat. The languid hours pass by on the shore — Alas for me!

The spring has done its flowering and taken leave. And now with the burden of faded futile flowers I wait and linger.

The waves have become clamorous, and upon the bank in the shady lane the yellow leaves flutter and fall.

What emptiness do you gaze upon! Do you not feel a thrill passing through the air with the notes of the faraway song floating from the other shore?

XXII

In the deep shadows of the rainy July, with secret steps, thou walkest, silent as night, eluding all watchers.

To-day the morning has closed its eyes, heedless of the insistent calls of the loud east wind, and a thick veil has been drawn over the ever-wakeful blue sky.

The woodlands have hushed their songs, and doors are all shut at every house. Thou art the solitary wayfarer in this deserted street. Oh, my only friend, my best beloved, the gates are open in my house — do not pass by like a dream.

XXIII

Art thou abroad on this stormy night on thy journey of love, my friend? The sky groans like one in despair.

I have no sleep to-night. Ever and again I open my door and look out on the darkness, my friend!

I can see nothing before me. I wonder where lies thy path!

By what dim shore of the ink-black river, by what far edge of the frowning forest, through what mazy depth of gloom art thou threading thy course to come to me, my friend?

XXIV

If the day is done, if birds sing no more, if the wind has flagged tired, then draw the veil of darkness thick upon me, even as thou hast wrapt the earth with the coverlet of sleep and tenderly closed the petals of the drooping lotus at dusk.

From the traveller, whose sack of provisions is empty before the voyage is ended, whose garment is torn and dust-laden, whose strength is exhausted, remove shame and poverty, and renew his life like a flower under the cover of thy kindly night.

XXV

In the night of weariness let me give myself up to sleep without struggle, resting my trust upon thee.

Let me not force my flagging spirit into a poor preparation for thy worship.

It is thou who drawest the veil of night upon the

tired eyes of the day to renew its sight in a fresher gladness of awakening.

XXVI

He came and sat by my side but I woke not. What a cursed sleep it was, 0 miserable me!

He came when the night was still; he had his harp in his hands, and my dreams became resonant with its melodies.

Alas, why are my nights all thus lost? Ah, why do I ever miss his sight whose breath touches my sleep?

XXVII

Light, oh, where is the light? Kindle it with the burning fire of desire!

There is the lamp but never a flicker of a flame, — is such thy fate, my heart? Ah, death were better by far for thee!

Misery knocks at thy door, and her message is that thy lord is wakeful, and he calls thee to the love-tryst through the darkness of night

The sky is overcast with clouds and the rain is ceaseless. I know not what this is that stirs in me, — I know not its meaning.

A moment's flash of lightning drags down a deeper gloom on my sight, and my heart gropes for the path to where the music of the night calls me.

Light, oh, where is the light? Kindle it with the burning fire of desire! It thunders and the wind rushes screaming through the void. The night is black as a black stone. Let not the hours pass by in the dark. Kindle the lamp of love with thy life.

XXVIII

Obstinate are the trammels, but my heart aches when I try to break them.

Freedom is all I want, but to hope for it I feel ashamed.

I am certain that priceless wealth is in thee, and that thou art my best friend, but I have not the heart to sweep away the tinsel that fills my room.

The shroud that covers me is a shroud of dust and death; I hate it, yet hug it in love.

My debts are large, my failures great, my shame secret and heavy; yet when I come to ask for my good, I quake in fear lest my prayer be granted.

XXIX

He whom I enclose with my name is weeping in this dungeon. I am ever busy building this wall all around; and as this wall goes up into the sky day by day I lose sight of my true being in its dark shadow.

I take pride in this great wall, and I plaster it with dust and sand lest a least hole should be left in this name; and for all the care I take I lose sight of my true being.

XXX

I came out alone on my way to my tryst But who is this that follows me in the silent dark?

I move aside to avoid his presence but I escape him not.

He makes the dust rise from the earth with his swagger; he adds his loud voice to every word that I utter.

He is my own little self, my lord, he knows no shame; but I am ashamed to come to thy door in his company.

XXXI

"Prisoner, tell me, who was it that bound you?"

"It was my master," said the prisoner. "I thought I could outdo everybody in the world in wealth and power, and I amassed in my own treasure-house the money due to my king. When sleep overcame me I lay upon the bed that was for my lord, and on waking up I found I was a prisoner in my own treasure-house."

"Prisoner, tell me, who was it that wrought this unbreakable chain?"

"It was I," said the prisoner, "who forged this chain very carefully. I thought my invincible power would hold the world captive leaving me in a freedom undisturbed. Thus night and day I worked at the chain with huge fires and cruel hard strokes. When at last the work was done and the links were complete and unbreakable, I found that it held me in its grip."

XXXII

By all means they try to hold me secure who love me in this world. But it is otherwise with thy love which is greater than theirs, and thou keepest me free.

Lest I forget them they never venture to leave me alone. But day passes by after day and thou art not seen.

If I call not thee in my prayers, if I keep not thee in my heart, thy love for me still waits for my love.

XXXIII

When it was day they came into my house and said, "We shall only take the smallest room here."

They said, "We shall help you in the worship of your God and humbly accept only our own share of his grace;" and then they took their seat in a corner and they sat quiet and meek.

But in the darkness of night I find they break into my sacred shrine, strong and turbulent, and snatch with unholy greed the offerings from God's altar.

XXXIV

Let only that little be left of me whereby I may name thee my all.

Let only that little be left of my will whereby I may feel thee on every side, and come to thee in everything, and offer to thee my love every moment

Let only that little be left of me whereby I may never hide thee.

Let only that little of my fetters be left whereby I am bound with thy will, and thy purpose is carried out in my life — and that is the fetter of thy love.

XXXV

Where the mind is without fear and the head is held high;

Where knowledge is free;

Where the world has not been broken up into fragments by narrow domestic walls;

Where words come out from the depth of truth;

Where tireless striving stretches its arms towards perfection;

Where the clear stream of reason has not lost its way into the dreary desert sand of dead habit;

Where the mind is led forward by thee into ever-widening thought and action —

Into that heaven of freedom, my Father, let my country awake.

XXXVI

This is my prayer to thee, my lord — strike, strike at the root of penury in my heart.

Give me the strength lightly to bear my joys and sorrows.

Give me the strength to make my love fruitful in service.

Give me the strength never to disown the poor or bend my knees before insolent might.

Give me the strength to raise my mind high above daily trifles.

And give me the strength to surrender my strength to thy will with love.

XXXVII

I thought that my voyage had come to its end at the last limit of my power, — that the path before me was closed, that provisions were exhausted and the time come to take shelter in a silent obscurity.

But I find that thy will knows no end in me. And when old words die out on the tongue, new melodies break forth from the heart; and where the old tracks are lost, new country is revealed with its wonders.

XXXVIII

That I want thee, only thee — let my heart repeat without end. All desires that distract me, day and night, are false and empty to the core.

As the night keeps hidden in its gloom the petition for light, even thus in the depth of my unconsciousness rings the cry — "I want thee, only thee".

As the storm still seeks its end in peace when it strikes against peace with all its might, even thus my rebellion strikes against thy love and still its cry is — "I want thee, only thee".

XXXIX

When the heart is hard and parched up, come upon me with a shower of mercy.

When grace is lost from life, come with a burst of song.

When tumultuous work raises its din on all sides shutting me out from beyond, come to me, my lord of silence, with thy peace and rest.

When my beggarly heart sits crouched, shut up in a corner, break open the door, my king, and come with the ceremony of a king.

When desire blinds the mind with delusion and dust, O thou holy one, thou wakeful, come with thy light and thy thunder.

XL

The rain has held back for days and days, my God, in my arid heart. The horizon is fiercely naked — not the thinnest cover of a soft cloud, not the vaguest hint of a distant cool shower.

Send thy angry storm, dark with death, if it is thy wish, and with lashes of lightning startle the sky from end to end.

But call back, my lord, call back this pervading silent heat, still and keen and cruel, burning the heart with dire despair.

Let the cloud of grace bend low from above like the tearful look of the mother on the day of the father's wrath.

XLI

Where dost thou stand behind them all, my lover, hiding thyself in the shadows? They push thee and pass thee by on the dusty road, taking thee for naught. I wait here weary hours spreading my offerings for thee, while passers-by come and take my flowers, one by one, and my basket is nearly empty.

The morning time is past, and the noon. In the shade of evening my eyes are drowsy with sleep. Men going home glance at me and smile and fill me with shame. I sit like a beggar maid, drawing my skirt over my face, and when they ask me what it is I want, I drop my eyes and answer them not

Oh, how, indeed, could I tell them that for thee I wait, and that thou hast promised to come? How could I utter for shame that I keep for my dowry this poverty? Ah, I hug this pride in the secret of my heart.

I sit on the grass and gaze upon the sky and dream of the sudden splendour of thy coming — all the lights ablaze, golden pennons flying over thy car, and they at the roadside standing agape, when they see thee come down from thy seat to raise me from the dust, and set at thy side this ragged beggar girl a-tremble with shame and pride, like a creeper in a summer breeze.

But time glides on and still no sound of the wheels of thy chariot. Many a procession passes by with noise and shouts and glamour of glory. Is it only thou who wouldst stand in the shadow silent and behind them all? And only I who would wait and weep and wear out my heart in vain longing?

XLII

Early in the day it was whispered that we should sail in a boat, only thou and I, and never a soul in the world would know of this our pilgrimage to no country and to no end.

In that shoreless ocean, at thy silently listening smile my songs would swell in melodies, free as waves, free from all bondage of words.

Is the time not come yet? Are there works still to do? Lo, the evening has come down upon the shore and in the fading light the seabirds come flying to their nests.

Who knows when the chains will be off, and the boat, like the last glimmer of sunset, vanish into the night?

XLIII

The day was when I did not keep myself in readiness for thee; and entering my heart unbidden even as one of the common crowd, unknown to me, my king, thou didst press the signet of eternity upon many a fleeting moment of my life.

And to-day when by chance I light upon them and see thy signature, I find they have lain scattered in the dust mixed with the memory of joys and sorrows of my trivial days forgotten.

Thou didst not turn in contempt from my childish play among dust, and the steps that I heard in my playroom are the same that are echoing from star to star.

XLIV

This is my delight, thus to wait and watch at the wayside where shadow chases light and the rain comes in the wake of the summer.

Messengers, with tidings from unknown skies, greet me and speed along the road. My heart is glad within, and the breath of the passing breeze is sweet.

From dawn till dusk I sit here before my door, and I know that of a sudden the happy moment will arrive when 1 shall see.

In the meanwhile I smile and I sing all alone. In the meanwhile the air is filling with the perfume of promise.

XLV

Have you not heard his silent steps? He comes, comes, ever comes.

Every moment and every age, every day and every night he comes, comes, ever comes. Many a song have I sung in many a mood of mind, but all their notes have always proclaimed, "He comes, comes, ever comes"

In the fragrant days of sunny April through the forest path he comes, comes, ever comes.

In the rainy gloom of July nights on the thundering chariot of clouds he comes, comes, ever comes.

In sorrow after sorrow it is his steps that press upon my heart, and it is the golden touch of his feet chat makes my joy to shine.

XLVI

I know not from what distant time thou art ever coming nearer to meet me. Thy sun and stars can never keep thee hidden from me for aye.

In many a morning and eve thy footsteps have been heard and thy messenger has come within my heart and called me in secret.

I know not why to-day my life is all astir, and a feeling of tremulous joy is passing through my heart.

It is as if the time were come to wind up my work, and I feel in the air a faint smell of thy sweet presence.

XLVII

The night is nearly spent waiting for him in vain. I fear lest in the morning he suddenly come to my door when I have fallen asleep wearied out. Oh, friends, leave the way open to him — forbid him not.

If the sound of his steps does not wake me, do not try to rouse me, I pray. I wish not to be called from my sleep by the clamorous choir, of birds, by the riot of wind at the festival of morning light. Let me sleep undisturbed even if my lord comes of a sudden to my door.

Ah, my sleep, precious sleep, which only waits for his touch to vanish. Ah, my closed eyes that would open their lids only to the light of his smile when he stands before me like a dream emerging from darkness of sleep.

Let him appear before my sight as the first of all lights and all forms. The first thrill of joy to my awakened soul, let it come from his glance. And let my return to myself be immediate return to him.

XLVIII

The morning sea of silence broke into ripples of bird songs; and the flowers were all merry by the roadside; and the wealth of gold was scattered through the rift of the clouds while we busily went on our way and paid no heed. We sang no glad songs nor played; we went not to the village for barter; we spoke not a word nor smiled; we lingered not on the way. We quickened our pace more and more as the time sped by.

The sun rose to the mid sky and doves cooed in the shade. Withered leaves danced and whirled in the hot air of noon. The shepherd boy drowsed and dreamed in the shadow of the banyan tree, and I laid myself down by the water and stretched my tired limbs on the grass.

My companions laughed at me in scorn; they held their heads high and hurried on; they never looked back nor rested; they vanished in the distant blue haze. They crossed many meadows and hills, and passed chrough strange, far-away countries. All honour to you, heroic host of the interminable path! Mockery and reproach pricked me ro rise, but found no response in me. I gave myself up for lost in the depth of a glad humiliation — in the shadow of a dim delight.

The repose of the sun-embroidered green gloom slowly spread over my heart. I forgot for what I had travelled, and I surrendered my mind without struggle to the maze of shadows and songs.

At last, when I woke from my slumber and opened my eyes, I saw thee standing by me, flooding my sleep with thy smile. How I had feared that the path was long and wearisome, and the struggle to reach thee was hard!

XLIX

You came down from your throne and stood at my cottage door.

I was singing all alone in a corner, and the melody caught your ear. You came down and stood at my cottage door.

Masters are many in your hall, and songs are sung there at all hours. But the simple carol of this novice struck at your love. One plaintive little strain mingled with the great music of the world, and with a flower for a prize you came down and stopped at my cottage door.

L

I had gone a-begging from door to door in the village path, when thy golden chariot appeared in the distance like a gorgeous dream and I wondered who was this King of all kings!

My hopes rose high and methought my evil days were at an end, and I stood waiting for alms to be given unasked and for wealth scattered on all sides in the dust.

The chariot stopped where I stood. Thy glance fell on me and thou camest down with a smile. I felt that the luck of my life had come at last. Then of a sudden thou didst hold out thy right hand and say, "What hast thou to give to me?"

Ah, what a kingly jest was it to open thy palm to a beggar to beg! I was confused and stood undecided, and then from my wallet I slowly cook out the least little grain of corn and gave it to thee.

But how great my surprise when at the day's end I emptied my bag on the floor to find a least little grain of gold among the poor heap! I bitterly wept and wished that I had had the heart to give thee my all.

LI

The night darkened. Our day's works had been done. We thought that the last guest had arrived for the night and the doors in the village were all shut. Only some said the King was to come. We laughed and said, "No, it cannot be!"

It seemed there were knocks at the door and we said it was nothing but the wind. We put out the lamps and lay down to sleep. Only some said, "It is the messenger!" We laughed and said, "No, it must be the wind!"

There came a sound in the dead of the night. We sleepily thought it was the distant thunder. The earth shook, the walls rocked, and it troubled us in our sleep. Only some said it was the sound of wheels. We said in a drowsy murmur, "No, it must be the rumbling of clouds!"

The night was still dark when the drum sounded. The voice came, "Wake up! delay not!" We pressed our hands on our hearts and shuddered with fear. Some said, "Lo, there is the King's flag!" We stood up on our feet and cried "There is no time for delay!"

The King has come — but where are lights, where are wreaths? Where is the throne to seat him? Oh, shame! Oh utter shame! Where is the hall, the decorations? Some one has said, "Vain is this cry! Greet him with empty hands, lead him into thy rooms all bare!"

Open the doors, let the conch-shells be sounded! In the depth of the night has come the King of our dark, dreary house. The thunder roars in the sky. The darkness shudders with lightning. Bring out thy tattered piece of mat and spread it in the courtyard. With the storm has came of a sudden our King of the fearful night.

LII

I thought I should ask of thee — but I dared not — the rose wreath thou hadst on thy neck. Thus I waited for the morning, when thou didst depart, to find a few fragments on the bed. And like a beggar I searched in the dawn only for a stray petal or two.

Ah me, what is it I find? What token left of thy love? It is no flower, no spices, no vase of perfumed water. It is thy mighty sword, flashing as a flame, heavy as a bolt of thunder. The young light of morning comes through the window and spreads itself upon thy bed. The morning bird twitters and asks, "Woman, what hast thou got?" No, it is no flower, nor spices, nor vase of perfumed water — it is thy dreadful sword.

I sit and muse in wonder, what gift is this of thine. I can find no place where to hide it. I am ashamed to wear it, frail as I am, and it hurts me when I press it to my bosom. Yet shall I bear in my heart this honour of the burden of pain, this gift of thine.

From now there shall be no fear left for me in this world, and thou shalt be victorious in all my strife. Thou hast left death for my companion and I shall crown him with my life. Thy sword is with me to cut asunder my bonds, and there shall be no fear left for me in the world.

From now I leave off all petty decorations. Lord of my heart, no more shall there be for me waiting and weeping in corners, no more coyness and sweetness of demeanour. Thou hast given me thy sword for adornment. No more doll's decorations for me!

LIII

Beautiful is thy wristlet, decked with stars and cunningly wrought in myriad-coloured jewels. But more beautiful to me thy sword with its curve of lightning like the outspread wings of the divine bird of Vishnu, perfectly poised in the angry red light of the sunset.

It quivers like the one last response of life in ecstasy of pain at the final stroke of death; it shines like the pure flame of being burning up earthly sense with one fierce flash.

Beautiful is thy wristlet, decked with starry gems; but thy sword, O lord of thunder, is wrought with uttermost beauty, terrible to behold or to think of.

LIV

I asked nothing from thee; I uttered not my name to thine ear. When thou took'st thy leave I stood silent. I was alone by the well where the shadow of the tree fell aslant, and the women had gone home with their brown earthen pitchers full to the brim. They called me and shouted, "Come with us, the morning is wearing on to noon." But I languidly lingered awhile lost in the midst of vague musings.

I heard nor thy steps as thou eamest. Thine eyes were sad when they fell on me; thy voice was tired as thou spokest low — "Ah, I am a thirsty traveller." I started up from my day-dreams and poured water from my jar on thy joined palms. The leaves rustled overhead; the cuckoo sang from the unseen dark, and perfume of *babla* flowers came from the bend of the road.

I stood speechless with shame when my name thou didst ask. Indeed, what had I done for thee to keep me in remembrance? But the memory that I could give water to thee to allay thy thirst will cling to my heart and enfold it in sweetness. The morning hour is late, the bird sings in weary notes, *neem* leaves rustle overhead and I sit and think and think.

LV

Languors upon your heart and the slumber is still on your eyes.

Has not the word come to you that the flower is reigning in splendour among thorns? Wake, oh, awaken! Let not the time pass in vain!

At the end of the stony path, in the country of virgin solitude, my friend is sitting all alone. Deceive him not. Wake, oh, awaken!

What if the sky pants and trembles with the heat of the midday sun — what if the burning sand spreads its mantle of thirst — Is there no joy in the deep of your heart? At every footfall of yours, will not the harp of the road break out in sweet music of pain?

LVI

Thus it is that thy joy in me is so full. Thus it is that thou hast come down to me. O thou lord of all heavens, where would be thy love if I were not?

Thou hast taken me as thy partner of all this wealth. In my heart is the endless play of thy delight In my life thy will is ever taking shape.

And for this, thou who art the King of kings hast decked thyself in beauty to captivate my heart. And for this thy love loses itself in the love of thy lover, and there art thou seen in the perfect union of two.

LVII

Light, my light, the world-filling light, the eye-kissing light, heart-sweetening light!

Ah, the light dances, my darling, at the centre of my

life; the light strikes, my darling, the chords of my love; the sky opens, the wind runs wild, laughter passes over the earth.

The butterflies spread their sails on the sea of light Lilies and jasmines surge up on the crest of the waves of light.

The light is shattered into gold on every cloud, my darling, and it scatters gems in profusion.

Mirth spreads from leaf to leaf, my darling, and gladness without measure. The heaven's river has drowned its banks and the flood of joy is abroad.

LVIII

Let all the strains of joy mingle in my last song — the joy that makes the earth flow over in the riotous excess of the grass, the joy that sets the twin brothers, life and death, dancing over the wide world, the joy that sweeps in with the tempest, shaking and waking all life with laughter, the joy that sits still with its tears on the open red lotus of pain, and the joy that throws everything it has upon the dust, and knows not a word.

LIX

Yes, I know, this is nothing but thy love, O beloved of my heart — this golden light that dances upon the leaves, these idle clouds sailing across the sky, this passing breeze leaving its coolness upon my forehead. The morning light has flooded my. eyes — this is thy message to my heart. Thy face is bent from above, thy eyes look down on my eyes, and my heart has touched thy feet.

LXIII

Thou hast made me known to friends whom I knew not Thou hast given me seats in homes not my own. Thou hast brought the distant near and made a brother of the stranger.

I am uneasy at heart when I have to leave my accustomed shelter; I forget that there abides the old in the new, and that there also thou abidest

Through birth and death, in this world or in others, wherever thou leadest me it is thou, the same, the one companion of my endless life who ever linkest my heart with bonds of joy to the unfamiliar.

When one knows thee, then alien there is none, then no door is shut Oh, grant me my prayer that I may never lose the bliss of the touch of the one in the play of the many.

LXIV

On the slope of the desolate river among tall grasses I asked her, "Maiden, where do you go, shading your lamp with your mantle? My house is all dark and lonesome, — lend me your light!" She raised her dark eyes for a moment and looked at my face through the dusk. "I have come to the river," she said, "to float my lamp on the stream when the daylight wanes in the west." I stood alone among tall grasses and watched the timid flame of her lamp uselessly drifting in the tide.

In the silence of gathering night I asked her, "Maiden, your lights are all lit — then where do you go with your lamp? My house is all dark and lonesome, — lend me your light." She raised her dark eyes on my face and stood for a moment doubtful. "I have come," she said at last, "to dedicate my lamp to the sky." I stood and watched her light uselessly burning in the void.

In the moonless gloom of midnight I asked her, "Maiden, what is your quest, holding the lamp near your heart? My house is all dark and lonesome, – lend me your light." She stopped for a minute and thought and gazed at my face in the dark. "I have brought my light," she said, "to join the carnival of lamps." I stood and watched her little lamp uselessly lost among lights.

LXV

What divine drink wouldst thou have, my God, from this overflowing cup of my life?

My poet, is it thy delight to see thy creation through my eyes and to stand at the portals of my ears silently to listen to thine own eternal harmony?

Thy world is weaving words in my mind and thy joy is adding music to them. Thou givest thyself to me in love and then feelest thine own entire sweetness in me.

LXVI

She who ever had remained in the depth of my being, in the twilight of gleams and of glimpses; she who never opened her veils in the morning light, will be my last gift to thee, my God, folded in my final song.

Words have wooed yet failed to win her; persuasion has stretched to her its eager arms in vain.

I have roamed from country to country keeping her in the core of my heart, and around her have risen and fallen the growth and decay of my life.

Over my thoughts and actions, my slumbers and dreams, she reigned yet dwelled alone and apart.

Many a man knocked at my door and asked for her and turned away in despair.

There was none in the world who ever saw her face to face, and she remained in her loneliness waiting for thy recognition.

LXVII

Thou art the sky and thou art the nest as well.

O thou beautiful, there in the nest it is thy love that encloses the soul with colours and sounds and odours.

There comes the morning with the golden basket in her right hand bearing the wreath of beauty, silently to crown the earth.

And there comes the evening over the lonely meadows deserted by herds, through trackless paths, carrying cool draughts of peace in her golden pitcher from the western ocean of rest.

But there, where spreads the infinite sky for the soul to take her flight in, reigns the stainless white radiance. There is no day nor night, nor form nor colour, and never, never a word.

LXVIII

Thy sunbeam comes upon this earth of mine with arms outstretched and stands at my door the livelong day to carry back to thy feet clouds made of my tears and sighs and songs.

With fond delight thou wrappest about thy starry breast that mantle of misty cloud, turning it into numberless shapes and folds and colouring it with hues everchanging.

It is so light and so fleeting, tender and tearful and dark, that is why thou lovest it, O thou spotless and serene. And that is why it may cover thy awful white light with its pathetic shadows.

LXIX

The same stream of life that runs through my veins night and day runs through the world and dances in rhythmic measures.

It is the same life that shoots in joy through the dust of the earth in numberless blades of grass and breaks into tumultuous waves of leaves and flowers.

It is the same life that is rocked in the ocean-cradle of birth and of death, in ebb and in flow.

I feel my limbs are made glorious by the touch of this world of life. And my pride is from the life-throb of ages dancing in my blood this moment

LXX

Is it beyond thee to be glad with the gladness of this rhythm? to be tossed and lost and broken in the whirl of this fearful joy?

All things rush on, they stop not, they look not behind, no power can hold them back, they rush on.

Keeping steps with that restless, rapid music, seasons come dancing and pass away — colours, tunes, and perfumes pour in endless cascades in the abounding joy that scatters and gives up and dies every moment.

LXXI

That I should make much of myself and turn it on all sides, thus casting coloured shadows on thy radiance — such is thy *maya*. Thou settest a barrier in thine own being and then callest thy severed self in myriad notes. This thy self-separation has taken body in me.

The poignant song is echoed through all the sky in many-coloured tears and smiles, alarms and hopes; waves rise up and sink again, dreams break and form. In me is thy own defeat of self.

This screen that thou hast raised is painted with innumerable figures with the brush of the night and the day. Behind it thy seat is woven in wondrous mysteries of curves, casting away all barren lines of straightness.

The great pageant of thee and me has overspread the sky. With the tune of thee and me all the air is vibrant, and all ages pass with the hiding and seeking of thee and me.

LXXII

He it is, the innermost one, who awakens my being with his deep hidden touches.

He it is who puts his enchantment upon these eyes and joyfully plays on the chords of my heart in varied cadence of pleasure and pain.

He it is who weaves the web of this *maya* in evanescent hues of gold and silver, blue and green, and lets peep out through the folds his feet, at whose touch I forget myself.

Days come and ages pass, and it is ever he who moves my heart in many a name, in many a guise, in many a rapture of joy and of sorrow.

LXXIII

Deliverance is not for me in renunciation. I feel the embrace of freedom in a thousand bonds of delight.

Thou ever pourest for me the fresh draught of thy wine of various colours and fragrance, filling this earthen vessel to the brim.

My world will light its hundred different lamps with thy flame and place them before the altar of thy temple.

No, I will never shut the doors of my senses. The delights of sight and hearing and touch will bear thy delight.

Yes, all my illusions will burn into illumination of joy, and all my desires ripen into fruits of love.

LXXIV

The day is no more, the shadow is upon the earth. It is time that I go to the scream to fill my pitcher.

The evening air is eager with the sad music of the water. Ah, it calls me out into the dusk. In the lonely lane there is no passer-by, the wind is up, the ripples are rampant in the river.

I know not if I shall come back home. I know not whom I shall chance to meet. There at the fording in the little boat the unknown man plays upon his lute.

LXXV

Thy gifts to us mortals fulfil all our needs and yet run back to thee undiminished.

The river has its everyday work to do and hastens through fields and hamlets; yet its incessant stream winds towards the washing of thy feet.

The flower sweetens the air with its perfume; yet its last service is to offer itself to thee.

Thy worship does not impoverish the world.

From the words of the poet men take what meanings please them; yet their last meaning points to thee.

LXXVI

Day after day, O lord of my life, shall I stand before thee face to face. With folded hands, O lord of all worlds, shall I stand before thee face to face.

Under thy great sky in solitude and silence, with humble heart shall I stand before thee face to face.

In this laborious world of thine, tumultuous with toil and with struggle, among hurrying crowds shall I stand before thee face to face.

And when my work shall be done in this world, 0 King of kings, alone and speechless shall I stand before thee face to face,

LXXVII

I know thee as my God and stand apart — I do not know thee as my own and come closer. I know thee as my father and bow before thy feet — I do not grasp thy hand as my friend's.

I stand not where thou comest down and ownest thyself as mine, there to clasp thee to my heart and take thee as my comrade.

Thou art the Brother amongst my brothers, but I heed them not, I divide not my earnings with them, thus sharing my all with thee.

In pleasure and in pain I stand not by the side of men, and thus stand by thee. I shrink to give up my life, and thus do not plunge into the great waters of life.

LXXVIII

When the creation was new and all the stars shone in their first splendour, the gods held their assembly in the sky and sang, "Oh, the picture of perfection! the joy unalloyed!"

But one cried of a sudden — "It seems that somewhere there is a break in the chain of light and one of the stars has been lost"

The golden string of their harp snapped, their song stopped, and they cried in dismay — "Yes, that lost star was the best, she was the glory of all heavens!"

From that day the search is unceasing for her, and the cry goes on from one to the other that in her the world has lost its one joy!

Only in the deepest silence of night the stars smile and whisper among themselves - "Vain is this seeking! Unbroken perfection is over all!"

LXXIX

If it is not my portion to meet thee in this my life then let me ever feel that I have missed thy sight — let me not forget for a moment, let me carry the pangs of this sorrow in my dreams and in my wakeful hours.

As my days pass in the crowded market of this world and my hands grow full with the daily profits, let me ever feel that I have gained nothing — let me not forget for a moment, let me carry the pangs of this sorrow in my dreams and in my wakeful hours.

When I sit by the roadside, tired and panting, when I spread my bed low in the dust, let me ever feel that the long journey is still before me — let me not forget for a moment, let me carry the pangs of this sorrow in my dreams and in my wakeful hours.

When my rooms have been decked out and the flutes sound and the laughter there is loud, let me ever feel that I have not invited thee to my house — let me not forget for a moment, let me carry the pangs of this sorrow in my dreams and in my wakeful hours.

LXXX

I am like a remnant of a cloud of autumn uselessly roaming in the sky, 0 my sun ever-glorious! Thy touch has not yet melted my vapour, making me one with thy light, and thus I count months and years separated from thee.

If this be thy wish and if this be thy play, then take this fleeting emptiness of mine, paint it with colours, gild it with gold, float it on the wanton wind and spread it in varied wonders.

And again when it shall be thy wish to end this play at night, I shall melt and vanish away in the dark, or it may be in a smile of the white morning, in a coolness of purity transparent.

LXXXI

On many an idle day have I grieved over lost time. But it is never lost, my lord. Thou hast taken every moment of my life in thine own hands.

Hidden in the heart of things thou art nourishing seeds into sprouts, buds into blossoms, and ripening flowers into fruitfulness.

I was tired and sleeping on my idle bed and imagined all work had ceased. In the morning I woke up and found my garden full with wonders of flowers.

LXXXII

Time is endless in thy hands, my lord. There is none to count thy minutes.

Days and nights pass and ages bloom and fade like flowers. Thou knowest how to wait

Thy centuries follow each other perfecting a small wild flower.

We have no time to lose, and having no time we must scramble for our chances. We are too poor to be late.

And thus it is that time goes by while I give it to every querulous man who claims it, and thine altar is empty of all offerings to the last

At the end of the day I hasten in fear lest thy gate be shut; but I find that yet there is time.

LXXXIII

Mother, I shall weave a chain of pearls for thy neck with my tears of sorrow.

The stars have wrought their anklets of light to deck thy feet, but mine will hang upon thy breast

Wealth and fame come from thee and it is for thee to give or to withhold them. But this my sorrow is absolutely mine own, and when I bring it to thee as my offering thou rewardest me with thy grace.

LXXXIV

It is the pang of separation that spreads throughout the world and gives birth to shapes innumerable in the infinite sky.

It is this sorrow of separation that gazes in silence all night from star to star and becomes lyric among rustling leaves in rainy darkness of July.

It is this overspreading pain that deepens into loves and desires, into sufferings and joys in human homes; and this it is that ever melts and flows in songs through my poet's heart.

LXXXV

When the warriors came out first from their master's hall, where had they hid their power?, Where were their armour and their arms?

They looked poor and helpless, and the arrows were showered upon them on the day they came out from their master's hall.

When the warriors marched back again to their master's hall, where did they hide their power?

They had dropped the sword and dropped the bow and the arrow; peace was on their foreheads, and they had left the fruits of their life behind them on the day they marched back again to their master's hall.

LXXXVI

Death, thy servant, is at my door. He has crossed the unknown sea and brought thy call to my home.

The night is dark and my heart is fearful — yet I will take up the lamp, open my gates and bow to him my welcome. It is thy messenger who stands at my door.

I will worship him with folded hands, and with tears. I will worship him placing at his feet the treasure of my heart.

He will go back with his errand done, leaving a dark shadow on my morning; and in my desolate home only my forlorn self will remain as my last offering to thee.

LXXXVII

In desperate hope I go and search for her in all the corners of my room; I find her not.

My house is small and what once has gone from it can never be regained.

But infinite is thy mansion, my lord, and seeking her I have come to thy door.

I stand under the golden canopy of thine evening sky and I lift my eager eyes to thy face.

I have come to the brink of eternity from which nothing can vanish – no hope, no happiness, no vision of a face seen through tears.

Oh, dip my emptied life into that ocean, plunge it into the deepest fullness. Let me for once feel that lost sweet touch in the allness of the universe.

LXXXVIII

Deity of the ruined temple! The broken strings of *Vina* sing no more your praise. The bells in the evening proclaim not your time of worship. The air is still and silent about you.

In your desolate dwelling comes the vagrant spring breeze. It brings the tidings of flowers — the flowers that for your worship are offered no more.

Your worshipper of old wanders ever longing for favour still refused. In the eventide, when fires and shadows mingle with the gloom of dust, he wearily comes back to the ruined temple with hunger in his heart

Many a festival day comes to you in silence, deity of the ruined temple. Many a night of worship goes away with lamp unlit.

Many new images are built by masters of cunning art and carried to the holy stream of oblivion when their time is come.

Only the deity of the ruined temple remains un-worshipped in deathless neglect.

LXXXIX

No more noisy, loud words from me – such is my master's will. Henceforth I deal in whispers. The speech of my heart will be carried on in murmurings of a song.

Men hasten to the King's market. All the buyers and sellers are there. But I have my untimely leave in the middle of the day, in the thick of work.

Let then the flowers come out in my garden, though it is not their time; and let the midday bees strike up their lazy hum.

Full many an hour have I spent in the strife of the good and the evil, but now it is the pleasure of my playmate of the empty days to draw my heart on to him; and I know not why is this sudden call to what useless inconsequence!

XC

on the day when death will knock at thy door what wilt thou offer to him?

Oh, I will set before my guest the full vessel of my life — I will never let him go with empty hands.

All the sweet vintage of all my autumn days and summer nights, all the earnings and gleanings of my busy life will I place before him at the close of my days when death will knock at my door.

XCI

O thou the last fulfilment of life, Death, my death, come and whisper to me!

Day after day have I kept watch for thee; for thee have I borne the joys and pangs of life.

All that I am, that I have, that I hope, and all my love have ever flowed towards thee in depth of secrecy. One final glance from thine eyes and my life will be ever thine own.

The flowers have been woven and the garland is ready for the bridegroom. After the wedding the bride shall leave her home and meet her lord alone in the solitude of night.

XCII

I know that the day will come when my sight of this earth shall be lost, and life will take its leave in silence, drawing the last curtain over my eyes.

Yet stars will watch at night, and morning rise as before, and hours heave like sea waves casting up pleasures and pains.

When I think of this end of my moments, the barrier of the moments breaks and I see by the light of death thy world with its careless treasures. Rare is its lowliest seat, rare is its meanest of lives.

Things that I longed for in vain and things that I got — let them pass. Let me but truly possess the things that I ever spurned and overlooked.

XCIII

I have got my leave. Bid me farewell, my brothers! I bow to you all and take my departure.

Here I give back the keys of my door — and I give up all claims to my house. I only ask for last kind words from you.

We were neighbours for long, but I received more than I could give. Now the day has dawned and the lamp that lit my dark corner is out. A summons has come and I am ready for my journey.

XCIV

At this time of my parting, wish me good luck, my friends! The sky is flushed with the dawn and my path lies beautiful.

Ask not what I have with me to take there. I start on my journey with empty hands and expectant heart. I shall put on my wedding garland. Mine is not the red-brown dress of the traveller, and though there are dangers on the way I have no fear in my mind.

The evening star will come out when my voyage is done and the plaintive notes of the twilight melodies be struck up from the King's gateway.

XCV

I was not aware of the moment when I first crossed the threshold of this life.

What was the power that made me open out into this vast mystery like a bud in the forest at – midnight?

When in the morning I looked upon the light I felt in a moment that I was no stranger in this world, that the inscrutable without name and form had taken me in irs arms in the form of my own mother.

Even so, in death the same unknown will appear as ever known to me. And because I love this life, I know I shall love death as well.

The child cries out when from the right breast the mother takes it away, in the very next moment to find in the left one its consolation.

XCVI

When I go from hence let this be my parting word, that what I have seen is unsurpassable.

I have tasted of the hidden honey of this lotus that expands on the ocean of light, and thus am I blessed — let this be my parting word.

In this playhouse of infinite forms I have had my play and here have I caught sight of him that is formless.

My whole body and my limbs have thrilled with his touch who is beyond touch; and if the end comes here, let it come — let this be my parting word.

XCVII

When my play was with thee I never questioned who thou wert. I knew nor shyness nor fear, my life was boisterous.

In the early morning thou wouldst call me from my sleep like my own comrade and lead me running from glade to glade.

On those days I never cared to know the meaning of songs thou sangest to me. Only my voice took up the tunes, and my heart danced in their cadence.

Now, when the playtime is over, what is this sudden sight that is come upon me? The world with eyes bent upon thy feet stands in awe with all its silent stars.

XCVIII

I will deck thee with trophies, garlands of my defeat. It is never in my power to escape unconquered.

I surely know my pride will go to the wall, my life will burst its bonds in exceeding pain, and my empty heart will sob out in music like a hollow reed, and the stone will melt in tears.

I surely know the hundred petals of a lotus will not remain dosed for ever and the secret recess of its honey will be bared.

From the blue sky an eye shall gaze upon me and summon me in silence. Nothing will be left for me, nothing whatever, and utter death shall I receive at thy feet

XCIX

When I give up the helm I know that the time has come for thee to take it. What there is to do will be instantly done. Vain is this struggle.

Then take away your hands and silently put up with your defeat, my heart, and think it your good fortune to sit perfectly still where you are placed.

These my lamps are blown out at every little puff of wind, and trying to light them I forget all else again and again.

But I shall be wise this time and wait in the dark, spreading my mat on the floor; and whenever it is thy pleasure, my lord, come silently and take thy seat here.

C

I dive down into the depth of the ocean of forms, hoping to gain the perfect pearl of the formless.

No more sailing from harbour to harbour with this my weather-beaten boat. The days are long past when my sport was to be tossed on waves.

And now I am eager to die into the deathless.

Into the audience hall by the fathomless abyss where swells up the music of toneless strings I shall take this harp of my life.

I shall tune it to the notes of for ever, and, when it has sobbed out its last utterance, lay down my silent harp at the feet of the silent

CI

Ever in my life have I sought thee with my songs. It was they who led me from door to door, and with them have I felt about me, searching and touching my world.

It was my songs that taught me all the lessons I ever learnt; they showed me secret paths, they brought before my sight many a star on the horizon of my heart.

They guided me all the day long to the mysteries of the country of pleasure and pain, and, at last, to what palace gate have they brought me in the evening at the end of my journey?

CII

I boasted among men that I had known you. They see your pictures in all works of mine. They come and ask me, "Who is he?" I know not how to answer them. I say, "Indeed, I cannot tell." They blame me and they go away in scorn. And you sit there smiling.

I put my tales of you into lasting songs. The secret gushes out from my heart. They come and ask me "Tell me all your meanings." I know not how to answer them. I say, "Ah, who knows what they mean!" They smile and go away in utter scorn. And you sit there smiling.

CIII

In one salutation to thee, my God, let all my sense spread out and touch this world at thy feet.

Like a rain-cloud of July hung low with its burden of unshed showers let all my mind bend down at thy door in one salutation to thee.

Let all my songs gather together their diverse strains into a single current and flow to a sea of silence in one salutation to thee.

Like a flock of homesick cranes flying night and day back to their mountain nests let all my life take its voyage to its eternal home in one salutation to thee.

- The End -